NEW BABY

Sarah Shaffi
& Isabel Otter

Illustrated by
Lucy Farfort

Bilal and Sofia are twins and
they do **everything** together.

The twins never mean to misbehave,
but sometimes trouble just seems to find them!

"Our mummy's got a bean in her tummy and it's going to turn into a baby!" says Bilal.

"It's not a bean, Bilal. It's an apple pip," says Sofia. "When the baby is ready, Ammi just has to press her tummy button and the baby will pop out."

Autumn soon blows into winter and the apple pip keeps growing!

"When Baby comes,
I'm going to share all
my favourite animals.
Even Otto the Owl,"
says Bilal.

"I'm going to
show the baby
how to make
rockets!" Sofia
says proudly.

Now, the apple pip is so big
that Ammi gets tired easily.

"Come on, Ammi.
Let's play tag."

"Be gentle," says Baba.
"Your ammi is carrying a precious load."

"All she ever does is snooze, now," says Sofia grumpily.

"Hush," says Baba. "Ammi is resting. Imagine if you had to carry a baby around with you all day. Don't you think you might get tired too?"

"No!"
say Sofia
and Bilal.

Baba laughs.
"We've got to look after Ammi.
Life will be different when the baby
comes. But, no matter what, we are
a family and that means we're a team."

The next morning, Baba wakes the twins with some big news!

"Hey, sleepyheads – it's time for me and Ammi to go to the hospital."

"The new baby will be here soon! Grandma and Grandpa will take care of you while we're away," says Baba.

"Don't worry, everything will be fine!" says Grandma.

Sofia and Bilal **know** that
they need to be patient.
And they **know** that they
are meant to be a team.

But, somehow, **doing** this
has become harder than ever…

"It's going to be a boy!"
shouts Bilal.

"No – a girl!"
Sofia shouts
back.

Grandpa says that
it doesn't matter whether
the baby is a girl or a boy.

The important thing is
who we are on the inside.

The next day, the twins go to meet their new sibling.

"This is your baby brother, Farhan.
His name means 'happiness
and laughter'," says Ammi.

For once,
Sofia and Bilal are
perfectly quiet.

Back at home,
life is **very** different.

The twins have
never had to share
Ammi and Baba
with anyone
before now.

"Why don't you come in and
show Farhan your boat and
rubber duck?" asks Baba.

Bilal and Sofia realise that sharing
is harder than they thought.

But some days, they all get along very well.

"Baba, can we make strawberry icing for Ammi's birthday cake?" asks Bilal.

Everything is going to plan until…

"It was just an accident," says Baba.
"Farhan is a baby. You must be patient
with him. Remember, we are a family
and that means we're a team."

"Sometimes things happen
that we can't control."

"What we can control is how
we react in those tricky
moments," says Ammi.

"Look at what we can achieve when
we all work together," Baba says.

The twins are hatching a plan.

Is there **mischief** in store?

"Happy Birthday, Ammi!
Farhan gave us the idea
to use our toys!"

"My wonderful family,"
Ammi smiles.
"We're a real…"

"…team!"
shout Bilal and Sofia.

Life has changed
and the family has
grown, but there
is still a place
for everyone.

Pool party!